Great River Regional Library
January 2020

JEWISH IMMIGRANTS
IN THEIR SHOES

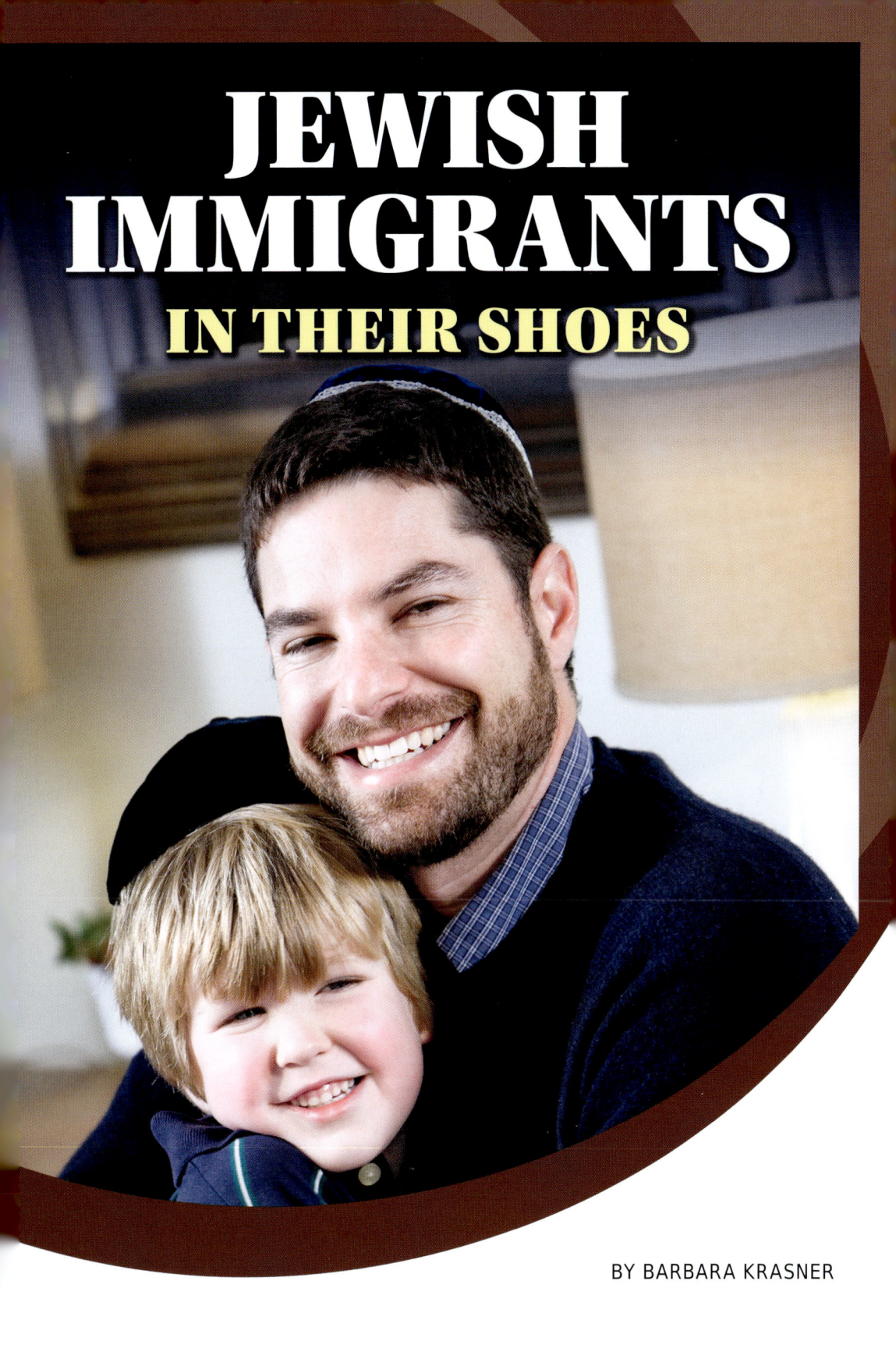

BY BARBARA KRASNER

Published by The Child's World®
1980 Lookout Drive • Mankato, MN 56003-1705
800-599-READ • www.childsworld.com

Content Consultant: Tobias Brinkmann, Associate Professor of Jewish Studies and History, Penn State University

Photographs ©: Golden Pixels LLC/Shutterstock Images, cover, 1; Everett Art/Shutterstock Images, 6; North Wind Picture Archives, 8, 10; iStockphoto, 9; Shutterstock Images, 12, 19, 28; GL Archive/Alamy, 13; Imagno/Hulton Archive/Getty Images, 15; Picture History/Newscom, 16, 20; Jewish Chronicle Heritage Images/Newscom, 18; Everett Historical/Shutterstock Images, 23; Laurent Gillieron/Keystone/AP Images, 24; Ben Margot/AP Images, 26

Copyright © 2019 by The Child's World®
All rights reserved. No part of this book may be reproduced or utilized in any form or by any means without written permission from the publisher.

ISBN 9781503827998
LCCN 2018944221

Printed in the United States of America
PA02394

ABOUT THE AUTHOR

Barbara Krasner is the author of more than 30 books for young readers. She teaches American immigrant history at several New Jersey universities.

TABLE OF CONTENTS

Fast Facts and Timeline 4

Chapter 1
Jews Arrive 6

Chapter 2
Opportunity Knocks 10

Chapter 3
For Safety and Freedom 16

Chapter 4
Escaping the Soviet Union 24

Think About It 29
Glossary 30
Source Notes 31
To Learn More 32
Index 32

FAST FACTS

Jews in the United States

- Jews came to the United States in part to escape the mistreatment they received because of their religion.
- Jews came to the United States from countries in South America, Europe, and the Middle East, depending on the time period.

Periods of Jewish Immigration

- Between 1820 and 1880, approximately 150,000 Jews came to the United States. Most of these immigrants were from German-speaking regions of Europe.
- Between 1880 and 1914, approximately two million Jews moved to the United States. Most came from Eastern Europe. They came for religious freedom and to escape poverty.
- After World War II (1939–1945), Jewish **refugees** who escaped the **Holocaust** resettled in the United States.

TIMELINE

- **1654:** Twenty-three Jewish refugees arrive in what is now the United States from Brazil.
- **1840s:** Jewish immigrants arrive from German-speaking lands.
- **1881:** Major Jewish immigration from Eastern Europe begins.
- **1921 and 1924:** U.S. Congress passes laws to severely restrict immigration.
- **1930s:** U.S. immigration restrictions prevent many German Jews from reaching the United States.
- **1940s and 1950s:** Jewish refugees from the Holocaust arrive.
- **1959:** Jews flee Cuba for the United States after the **communists** come to power.
- **1970s and 1980s:** Jewish refugees from the Soviet Union arrive.
- **1979:** Iranian Jews flee to the United States after the overthrow of Iran's government.

Chapter 1

JEWS ARRIVE

As the ship teetered on the dark waters of the harbor, four men, six women, and 13 children gathered up their belongings. They stepped onto the ship's deck and into the sunlight. They hurried to leave the ship. The Dutch port of New Amsterdam, which is present-day New York City, lay before them. They had risked their lives to come here from Brazil. It was no longer safe for Jews in Brazil. The new Portuguese governor didn't like Jews.

◀ **New Amsterdam was established in the 1620s.**

He had forced all Jews to either abandon their religion or leave by March 1654. If they didn't, they would be killed.

But now, even six months later, their freedom would have to wait. The ship's captain would not let the refugees leave the ship until they paid him a large sum that they couldn't afford. He instructed his crew to take some of the refugees' possessions to the market. But even selling what few belongings the Jews had left could not pay off the debt. Not satisfied, the captain held two Jews, David Israel Faro and Mose Lumbroso, responsible for the fate of all the Jews on board. The captain instructed the crew to put the two men in jail.

Fortunately, two newly arrived Jews from Europe came to their aid. Solomon Pietersen and Jacob Barsimson helped the refugees get money from friends and family in Europe. By the end of October, the Jews could finally leave the ship. They looked around at their new home. New Amsterdam was a busy port between the wilderness and the ocean. Fruit and vegetable peddlers crowded the port. There were pigs everywhere. The refugees saw a church, a storehouse, and a city hall. They heard many languages. They knew New Amsterdam could be a great place for them to live as merchants and traders.

▲ **New Amsterdam was a bustling city in the 1600s.**

However, the man in charge of the area, Peter Stuyvesant, did not want the Jews to settle in New Amsterdam. He refused to grant the Jews freedom of speech, the right to work, and freedom to worship. He wanted the Jews to leave. The Dutch West India Company, which had established New Amsterdam, sided with the Jews. The company's directors told Stuyvesant he had to grant the Jews the same rights as all other residents of New Amsterdam.

Meanwhile, more Jews arrived in New Amsterdam from Europe. The new Jewish community wrote **petitions** to gain their freedoms. Stuyvesant reluctantly granted the Jews the right to work and own property. Many Jews became successful merchants and traders with other parts of North America, the West Indies, and Europe.

▲ **Peter Stuyvesant was put in charge of all areas controlled by the Dutch in North America in 1646.**

Chapter 2

OPPORTUNITY KNOCKS

Abraham Kohn flipped to a new page in his diary. He carefully smoothed the paper before him and began writing, "It was difficult for me to leave my dear brothers and sisters, and especially, my beloved mother," he wrote, then paused.[1] A soft orange glow from the desk lamp lit the room. He thought of his home, the village he had left behind in Bavaria. This area would eventually become a southern region of Germany.

◀ **Immigrants traveling to the United States on ships often lived in crowded conditions.**

Kohn and his brother Moses had left the day before, on June 15, 1842, to seek their fortunes in the United States. They had been unable to find work in Bavaria. Their brother, Juda, wanted them to join him in North America.

It would be a long journey for the Kohn brothers. The pair traveled 366 miles (590 km) to the city of Bremen in Germany, mostly by foot and then carriage. On July 12, they sailed out to sea from the nearby port of Bremerhaven. Kohn felt a wave of excitement and nervousness as the ship sailed away. He wrote, "Farewell! The last glimpse of land, the German soil, brought mixed feelings."[2]

More than a month later, Kohn was still on the ship. He stood on deck and saw the ocean stretching endlessly before him. He was tired of the bland food and his uncomfortable bed. On August 24, he wrote, "How long, we wonder, must we remain at sea, waiting in vain to enter the calm harbor of New York? We grow ill and weary in addition with the terrible hot weather."[3]

Kohn grew more homesick each day, but on September 3, 1842, he saw his first glimpse of the United States' coast. As the ship approached New York, Kohn could make out buildings that stood near the shore. He also saw the vibrant green of the trees.

▲ Bavaria joined the German Empire in 1871.

He was ready to stand on solid ground again, but all the passengers were **quarantined** until they passed a medical inspection.

Once in New York, Kohn observed, "I enjoyed my first sight of the city immensely, but . . . I felt somewhat uncomfortable. The frantic hurry of the people, the hundreds of cabs, wagons, and carts—the noise is indescribable."[4] He tried to get a position as a clerk. But he soon realized he would have to become a peddler.

▲ **Some immigrants, beginning in the late 1800s, were quarantined on Hoffman Island in New York City.**

He had to haul a sack of merchandise on his back and sell door to door. A clerk was a more respected position than a peddler.

Kohn hated being a peddler. But he did not think about returning to Europe. Instead, he moved to Chicago, Illinois. Within two years of his arrival in the United States, he became a successful merchant there. He joined the Republican Party in Chicago and was elected to city clerk in 1860. Because Kohn was active in politics, he met Abraham Lincoln.

Between 1820 and 1880, the United States attracted young Jews like Kohn from German-speaking regions of Europe. They left mostly for economic reasons. They settled along the East Coast, in the Midwest, and in the South.

> "You have left your friends and acquaintances, your relatives and your parents, your home and your fatherland, your language and your customs, your faith and your religion—only to sell your wares in the wild places of America, in isolated farmhouses and tiny hamlets."[5]
>
> —Abraham Kohn in 1842 after arriving in New York

▶ Some Jewish immigrants received help from the Hebrew Immigrant Aid Society when they arrived in the United States.

14

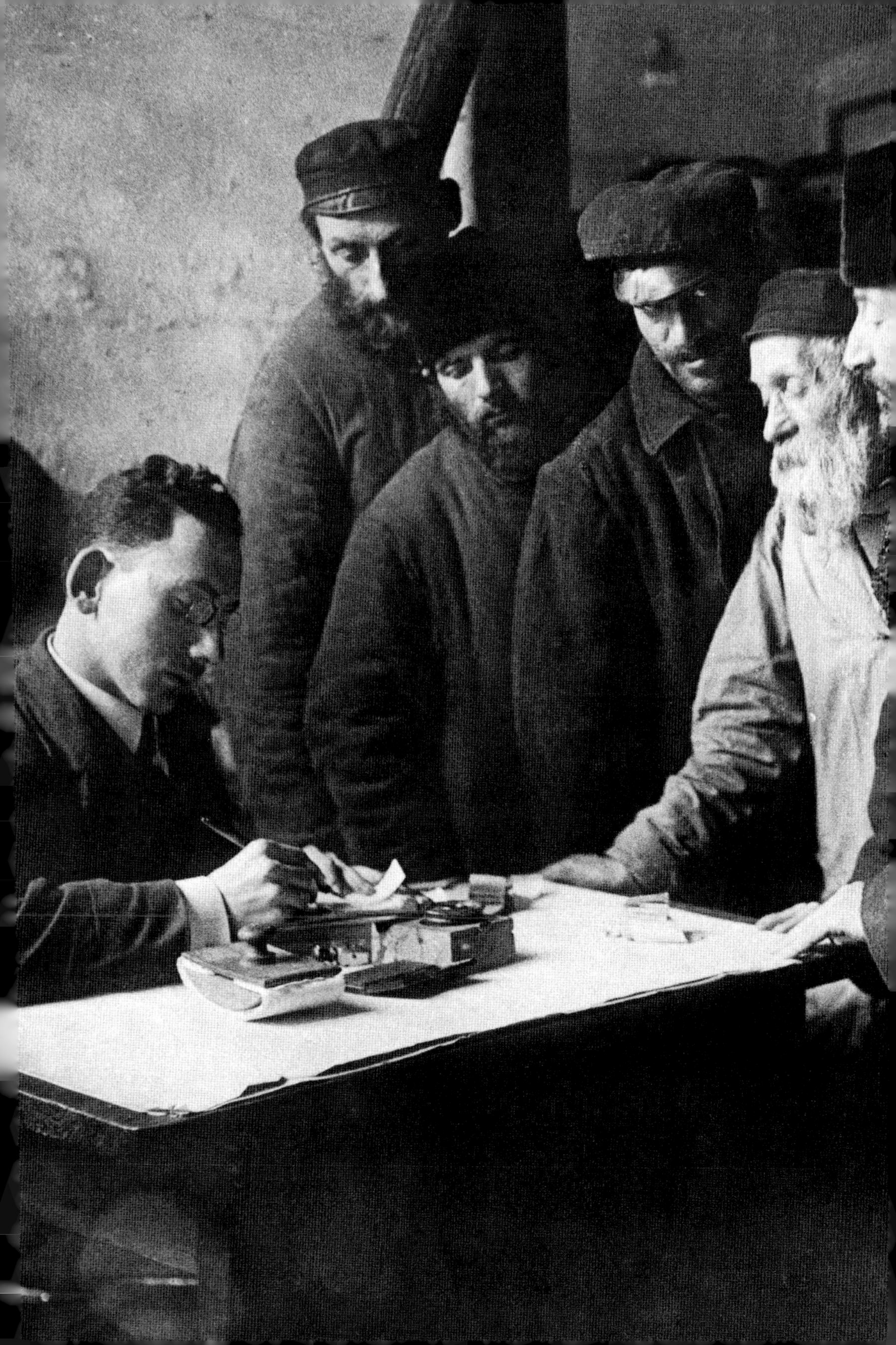

Chapter 3

FOR SAFETY AND FREEDOM

Talk of North America filled eight-year-old Mashke Antin's ears. She sat in the kitchen in her home in Plotzk, Russia. It was 1891. She listened as her father paced confidently in front of the family. He announced the time had come to leave their home. He would go to North America first, and when he settled and earned money, he would send for the rest of the family.

◀ **Mashke Antin, known as author Mary Antin in the United States, published her book *The Promised Land* in 1912.**

The day her father left, people crowded the train station to bid farewell. He said, "Good-bye, Plotzk, forever!"[6] Mashke watched him waving his hat from the train until he disappeared in the distance. Mashke imagined the day that she would follow her father. She was ready to leave the difficult life in Russia. She believed once she left, there would be no more wondering where the next meal would come from. She also hoped there would be no more harsh taxes for Jews and no more **pogroms**.

Her father wrote home when he could. His first letter trembled in Mashke's hands as she read it. She could hear his passion for the United States within each word. Mashke later wrote, "My father was inspired by a vision. He saw something—he promised us something. It was this 'America.' And 'America' became my dream."[7] Mashke waited three years to go to the United States. Then her father finally sent for her, her mother, her two sisters, and her brother to join him in Boston, Massachusetts.

But Mashke's family ran into trouble on their train at the Russian-German border. German border guards told them they would have to return to their home in Russia. Mashke was heartbroken. She missed her father. She wrote, "We were homeless, houseless, and friendless in a strange place."[8]

17

▲ **Some Jewish religious texts were destroyed in Russian pogroms.**

After a few days, while staying in a town near the border, her mother convinced authorities they should be allowed to enter Germany. The family was still determined to get to the United States. Finally, they reached the port city of Hamburg, Germany. Mashke was nervous, and she nibbled on the meager food her family had brought from home.

They waited more than a week for their ship to depart. It was **Passover**, and when it was time to board the ship, they were able to get some matzoh for their journey. Matzoh is a flat bread and is usually eaten during Passover. The trip across the Atlantic Ocean to Boston lasted 16 days. Mashke wrote, "And so suffering, fearing, brooding, rejoicing we crept nearer and nearer to the coveted shore, until, on a glorious May morning . . . our eyes beheld the Promised Land, and my father received us in his arms."[9]

▲ **Jews eat matzoh during the eight days of Passover.**

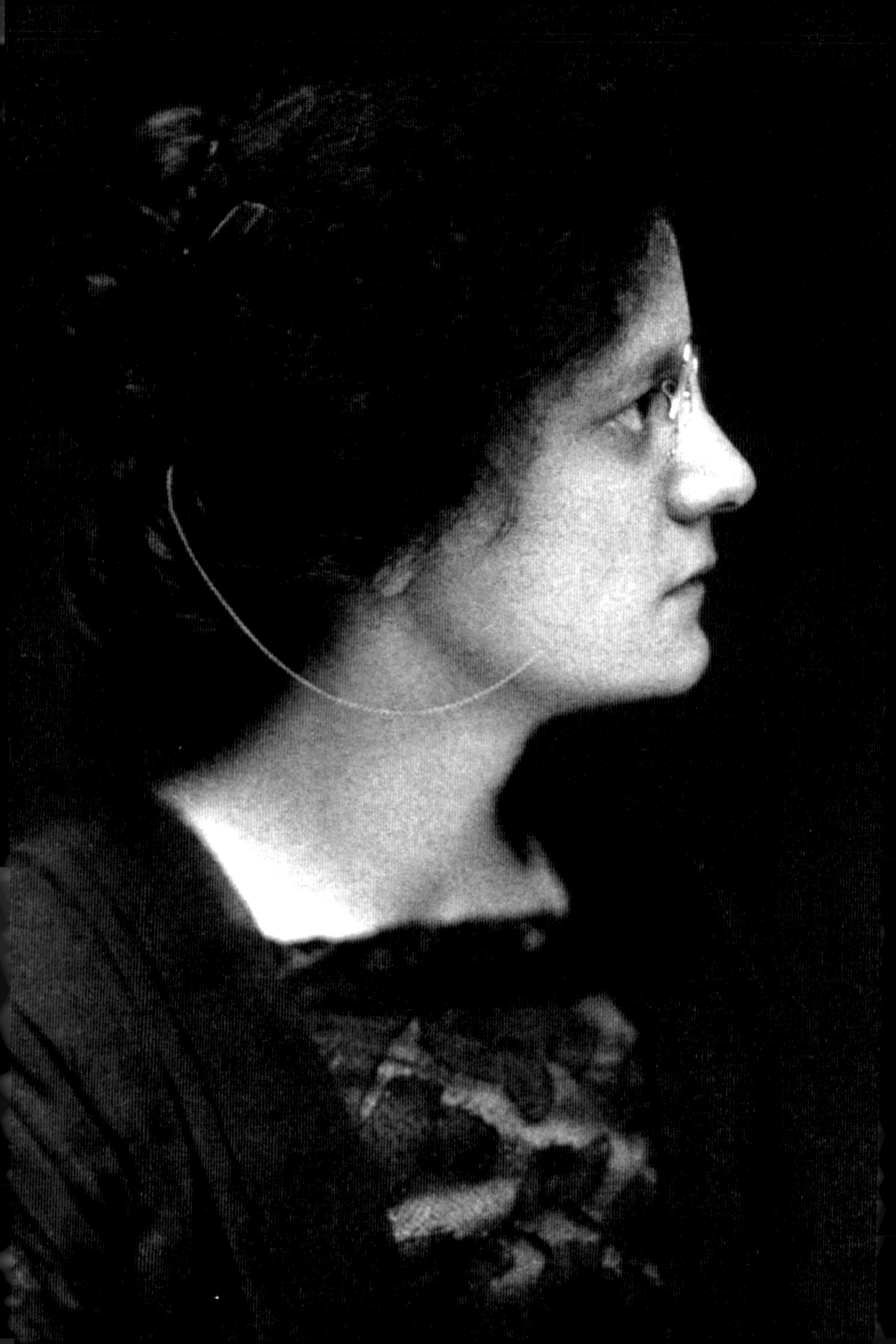

In Boston, Mashke marveled at brick buildings and streets. It was different from the dirt or wooden streets back home. Many of the foods were new to Mashke, especially canned food and a strange, slippery fruit called a banana.

More than anything, Mashke longed to be a real American. She felt she had to change some things about herself. Mashke recalled, "With our despised immigrant clothing we shed also our impossible Hebrew names."[10] Friends decided Mashke's name should be Mary. Although there were changes, Mashke was excited for life in the United States. Back in Russia, Jewish girls did not go to school. But in the United States, Mashke could. She learned quickly. Her teacher praised her English writing, even after only four months. Mashke's dream was to become a writer. Mashke published books about her immigrant experience.

"I looked up to the topmost row of windows, and my eyes were filled with the May blue of an American sky!"[11]

—Mashke Antin on her first day in Boston, 1894

◀ **Mashke's first book, *From Plotzk to Boston*, was about her experience coming to the United States as an immigrant.**

When World War I (1914–1918) broke out, it became difficult, if not impossible, for the Jews of Eastern Europe to leave. Tens of thousands lost their homes during the war. Others were murdered between 1918 and 1919 as civil war broke out in Russia. Also, in 1921 and 1924, new U.S. immigration laws restricted the number of people who could enter the country. These laws severely limited the number of eastern Europeans admitted.

In Adolf Hitler's **Nazi** Germany, anti-Jewish laws were introduced in 1933. These laws grew increasingly stricter, and many Jews were in danger. But they had few options about where to go. Six million Jews throughout Europe were murdered by the Nazis. After this mass killing and World War II, the United States opened its doors to Jewish refugees.

**European Jews were ordered into horrific camps by the Nazis. ▶
Many died from starvation, exposure, and exhaustion.**

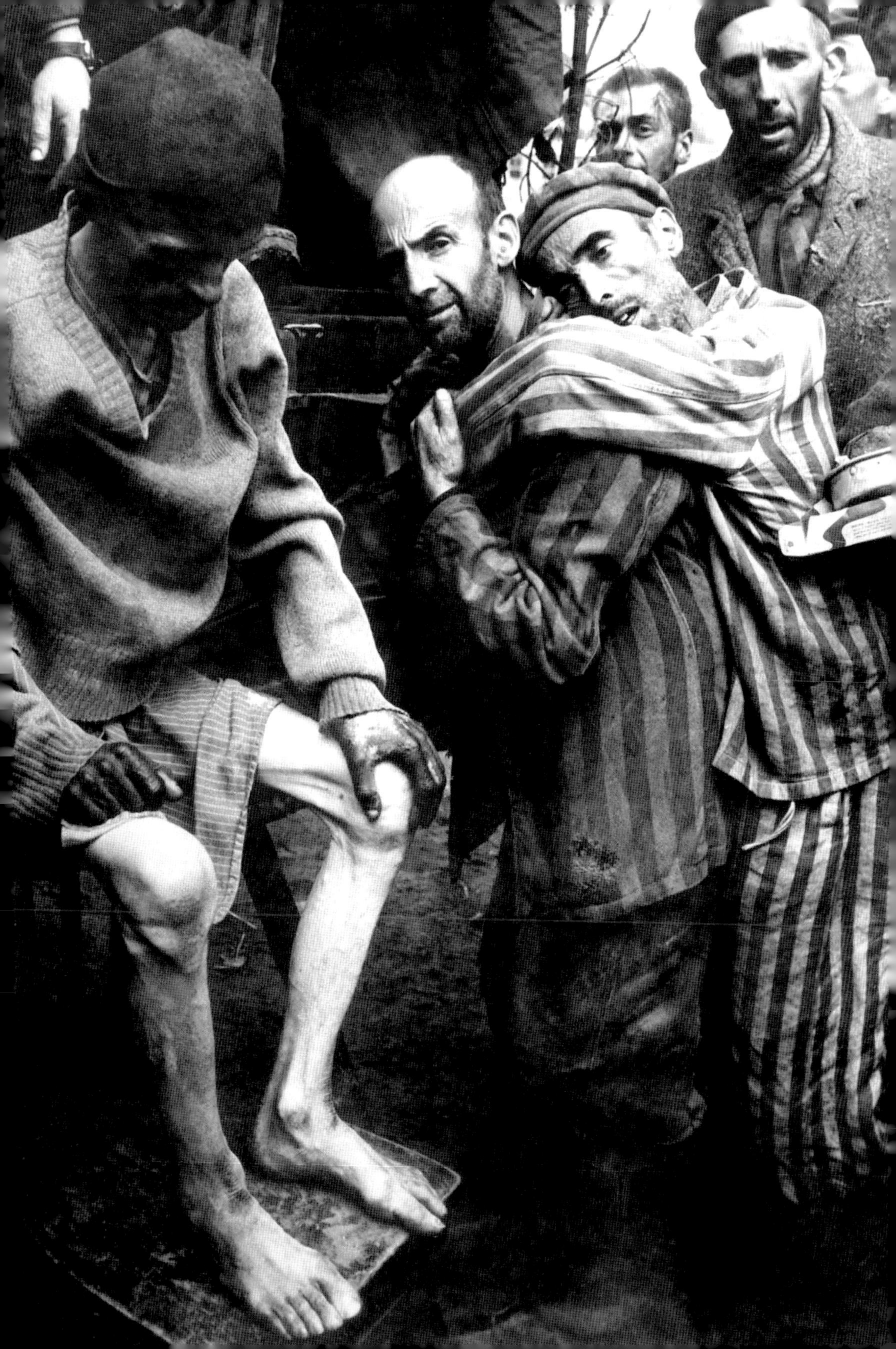

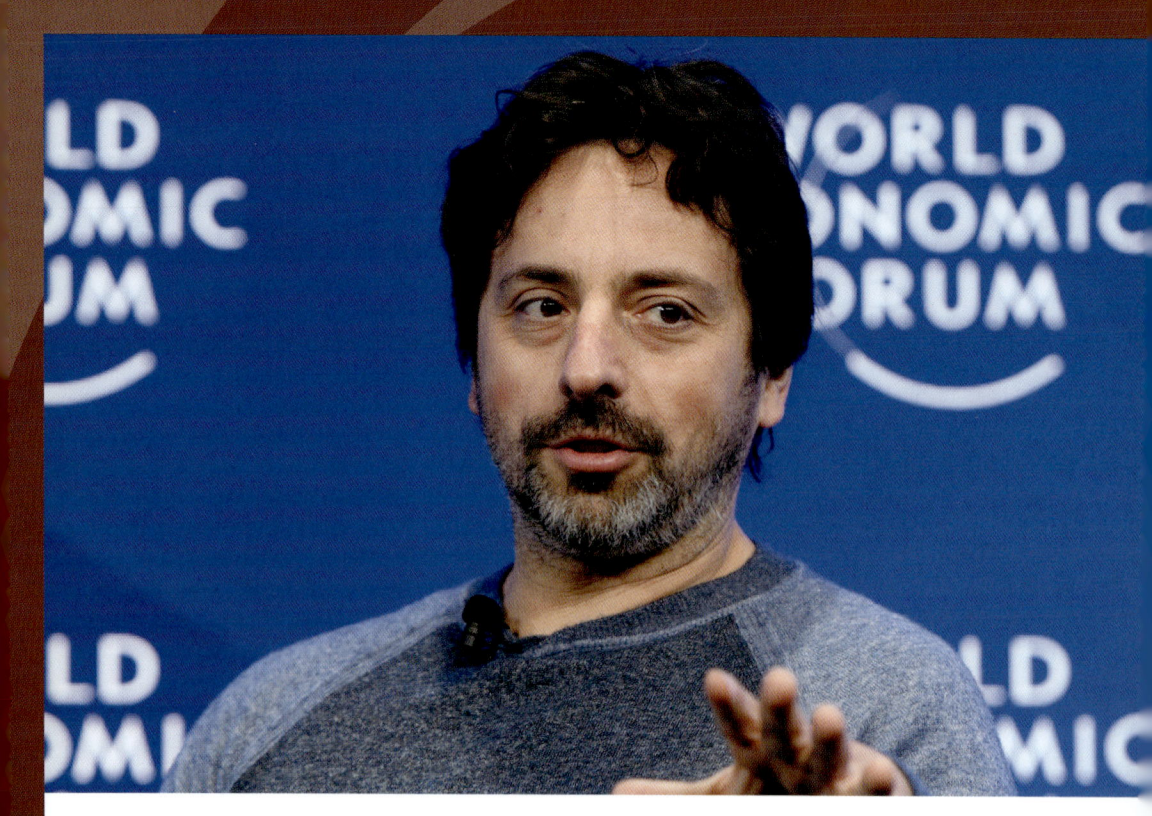

Chapter 4

ESCAPING THE SOVIET UNION

In the summer of 1977, four-year-old Sergey Brin waited at the door of his family's tiny three-room apartment in Moscow, Soviet Union. His father, Michael, had been away at a mathematics conference in Warsaw, Poland. When Michael burst through the door upon coming home, he announced it was time for the Brins to leave the Soviet Union.

◀ **Sergey Brin took advantage of opportunities in the United States.**

In Warsaw, Michael met people from the United States, England, France, and Germany. They were not the monsters Soviet authorities made them out to be. These people had spoken of limitless possibilities outside of the Soviet Union. Michael wanted that for himself, his wife, Eugenia, and Sergey.

Sergey's parents knew all too well the limitations of being Jewish in the Soviet Union. Michael had had to give up his dream of becoming an astronomer because he was Jewish. Soviet universities allowed only a small percentage of Jewish students to attend. Michael wanted Sergey to study whatever he wanted and wherever he wanted. Leaving the Soviet Union would bring risks. Even applying for **exit visas** could cause them to lose their jobs. Eugenia didn't think immigration was worth it. Michael finally convinced her that they had to leave for Sergey's sake.

Michael applied for their exit visas in September 1978. As expected, the couple lost their jobs. They each took whatever jobs they could get. Their exit visas finally arrived in May 1979. By this time, even young Sergey was eager to leave. He knew he did not fit in. He was not Russian. He was not welcome because he was Jewish.

For Sergey, now six, leaving the Soviet Union was a blur. He remembered, "We were in different places from day to day."[12] He found the constant movement unsettling. The family decided to go to the United States. The Brins flew to New York.

▲ **Sergey Brin (bottom) and Larry Page established Google in 1998.**

JEWISH IMMIGRATION TO THE UNITED STATES

Years	Number of Immigrants
1881-1898	533,478
1899-1907	829,244
1908-1924	1,008,586
1925-1931	73,378

Sergey's first memory of the United States came from the backseat of a car, which was whisking the family to Long Island, New York. He had never before seen such large cars.

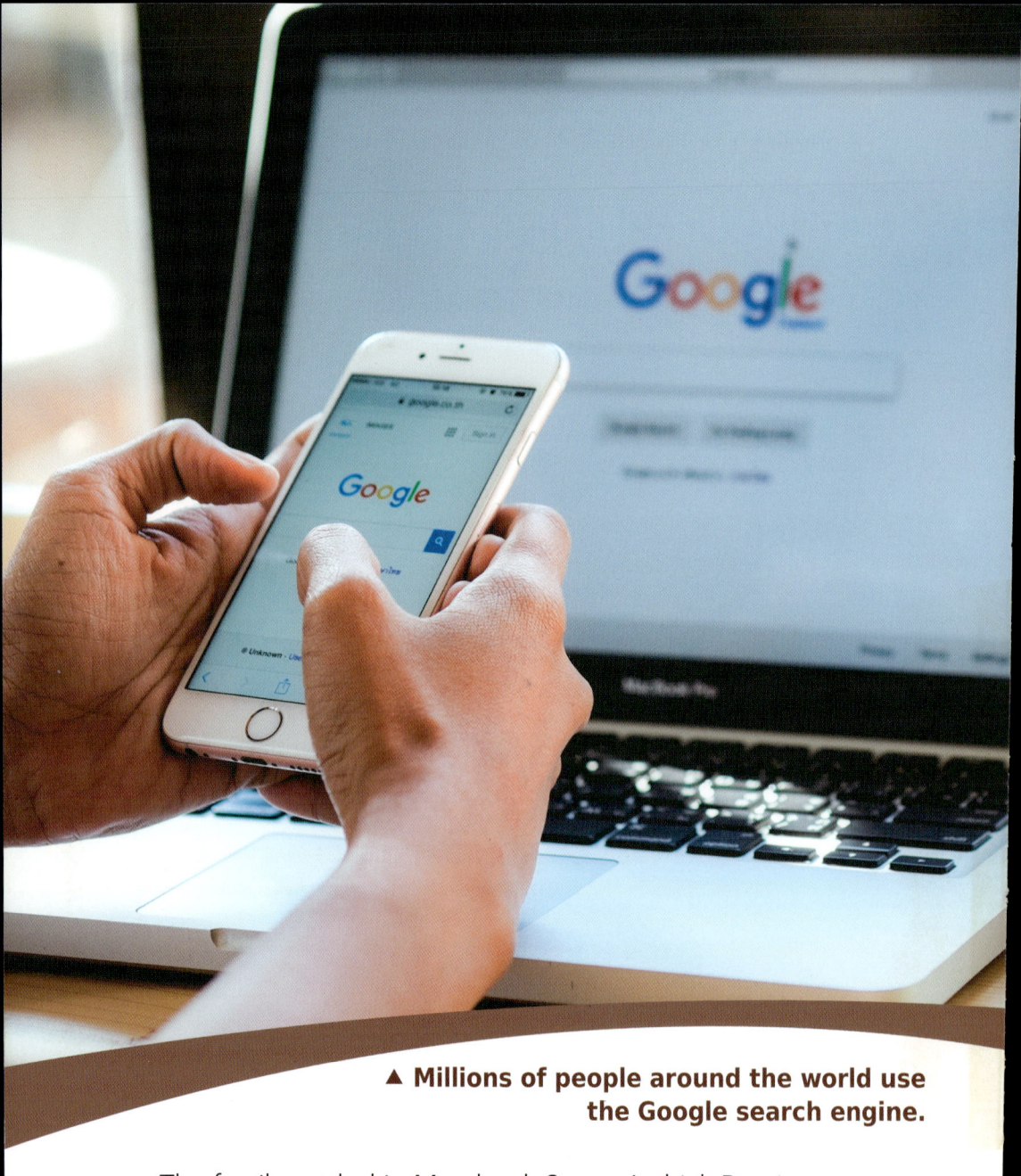

▲ **Millions of people around the world use the Google search engine.**

The family settled in Maryland. Sergey's thick Russian accent made it hard for him to make friends. His parents signed him up for elementary school. Sergey thrived in this environment. He became fascinated with numbers and puzzles.

Sergey went on to cofound the internet search company Google. Sergey told Google employees in 2017 that when he came to the country, "the [United States] had the courage to take me and my family in as refugees."[13] In 2017, he was the wealthiest immigrant in the United States. He was also one of the richest people in the world. However, Sergey never forgot that he arrived in the United States as an immigrant.

THINK ABOUT IT

- Why do you think some governments have restricted Jewish people's access to opportunities?
- Many Jewish people left their home countries to escape mistreatment and find better opportunities. Why did so many of them come to the United States?
- Why is it important to learn about the struggles that immigrants faced in the United States?

GLOSSARY

communists (KOM-you-nists): Communists are people who believe the state should control economic production. Communists took over the government of Russia in 1917.

exit visas (EK-sit VEE-zuhz): Exit visas are documents allowing people to leave their countries. Jews needed exit visas to leave the Soviet Union.

Holocaust (HAH-luh-kawst): The Holocaust is the name given to the intentional killing of six million Jews by the Nazis during World War II. Many Holocaust survivors came to the United States.

Nazi (NAHT-see): A Nazi was a member of the political party that governed Germany between 1933 and 1945. Nazi Germany passed anti-Jewish laws.

Passover (PAS-oh-vur): Passover is an eight-day Jewish holiday that celebrates the Israelites' escape from Egypt in Biblical times. Jews eat matzoh during Passover.

petitions (puh-TISH-uhns): Petitions are letters signed by people to ask authority figures to change their policies. Jews wrote petitions asking for freedoms.

pogroms (poh-GRUHMZ): Pogroms are hateful and violent acts against a specific group of people. Pogroms in Russia caused some Jews to leave.

quarantined (KWOR-uhn-teened): To be quarantined is to be kept away from others for a while to stop the spread of a disease. Immigrants were often quarantined upon their arrival in the United States.

refugees (ref-yoo-JEEZ): Refugees are people who seek safety in a foreign country, especially to avoid war or other dangers. Jewish refugees came to the United States.

SOURCE NOTES

1. Abram Vossen Goodman. "A Jewish Peddler's Diary." *American Jewish Archives*. The Jacob Rader Marcus Center of the American Jewish Archives, n.d. Web. 25 May 2018.

2. Ibid.

3. Ibid.

4. Ibid.

5. Ibid.

6. Mary Antin. *From Plotzk to Boston*. Boston, MA: W.B. Clarke, 1899. Print. 12.

7. Mary Antin. *The Promised Land*. Boston, MA: Houghton Mifflin Company, 1912. Print. 142–143.

8. Mary Antin. *From Plotzk to Boston*. Boston, MA: W.B. Clarke, 1899. Print. 25.

9. Mary Antin. *The Promised Land*. Boston, MA: Houghton Mifflin Company, 1912. Print. 179.

10. Ibid. 187–188.

11. Ibid. 184.

12. Mark Malseed. "The Story of Sergey Brin." *Moment*. Moment Magazine, 6 May 2013. Web. 25 May 2018.

13. Matt Weinberger. "'Outraged by This Order'—Here's the Speech Google Cofounder Sergey Brin Just Gave Attacking Trump's Immigration Ban." *Business Insider*. Insider, 30 Jan. 2017. Web. 25 May 2018.

TO LEARN MORE

Books

Golabek, Mona. *The Children of Willesden Lane: A True Story of Hope and Survival During World War II*. New York, NY: Little, Brown and Company, 2017.

Pressberg, Dava. *Anti-Semitism: Jewish Immigrants Seek Safety in America (1881–1914)*. New York, NY: PowerKids Press, 2016.

Zapruder, Alexandra. *Anne Frank*. Washington, DC: National Geographic, 2013.

Web Sites

Visit our Web site for links about Jewish immigrants: childsworld.com/links

Note to Parents, Teachers, and Librarians: We routinely verify our Web links to make sure they are safe and active sites. So encourage your readers to check them out!

INDEX

Antin, Mashke, 16, 17, 18, 19, 21

Bavaria, 10, 11

Brin, Sergey, 24, 25, 26, 27, 28, 29

Congress, 5

Dutch West India Company, 8

exit visas, 25

Google, 29

Hitler, Adolf, 22

Holocaust, 4, 5

Kohn, Abraham, 10, 11, 12, 13, 14

Lincoln, Abraham, 14

matzoh, 19

New Amsterdam, 6, 7, 8, 9

Passover, 19

peddlers, 7, 13, 14

pogroms, 17

quarantine, 12

refugees, 4, 5, 7, 22, 29

Soviet Union, 5, 25, 26

World War I, 22

World War II, 4, 22